This book belongs to:

....

....

For Serena, the original Little Bear, and Mom,
for her love and inspiration ~ SQ

Here's to a wonderful and colorful year of spending
time in the company of good friends and family ~ CP

An Imprint of Sterling Publishing
1166 Avenue of The Americas
New York, NY, 10036

SANDY CREEK and the distinctive Sandy Creek logo are registered trademarks of Barnes & Noble, Inc.

Text © 2013 by QED Publishing, Inc.
Illustrations © 2013 by QED Publishing, Inc.

This 2014 edition published by Sandy Creek.

ISBN 978-1-4351-5922-8

Manufactured in Guandong, China
Lot #:
2 4 6 8 10 9 7 5 3
12/15

Editor: Alexandra Koken
Designer: Verity Clark
Publisher: Zeta Jones

Little Bear
and the
Butterflies

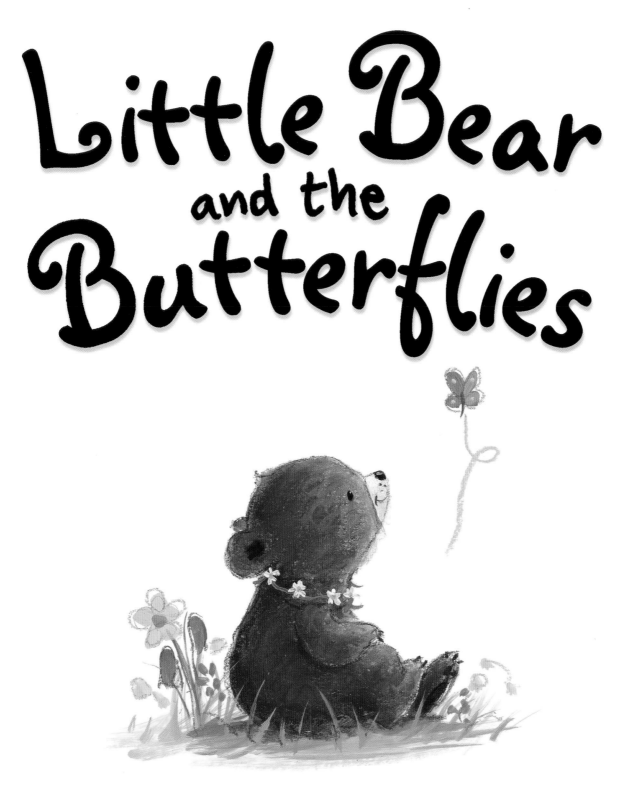

Susan Quinn and Caroline Pedler

Sandy Creek
NEW YORK

Little Bear was trying to
catch a butterfly.

"When I was little, chasing butterflies in Bluebell Meadow was my favorite game," said Mommy Bear.

Little Bear yawned.
"Can I go to Bluebell Meadow?"

"Later," said Mommy Bear.
"But now it's time for your nap."

Little Bear was almost asleep
when something tickled her nose.

It was a butterfly!

Little Bear stood up
and stretched.

She followed the
butterfly along the riverbank
and into the woods.

Little Bear tripped over a
tree root and landed on
her bottom.

"Watch out!"
shouted Rabbit.

"I was following a butterfly to Bluebell Meadow," Little Bear said. "But now the butterfly has gone."

"I'd like to go to Bluebell Meadow too," said Rabbit. "Let's see if Mouse knows the way."

"Oh, hello," said Mouse.
"I'm just piling up leaves to
bounce on. Would you like
to help me?"

"We'd love to," said Little Bear.
Soon there was a mountain
of leaves higher than
Mouse and Rabbit.

"This is fun!"
they squealed,
bouncing up
and down.

"Now we need to find Bluebell Meadow,"
Little Bear explained to Mouse.

"Let's ask Owl," said Mouse.
"He knows everything."

So Little Bear
climbed Owl's tree...

"I'm trying to sleep!"
grumbled Owl.

"Sorry," said Little Bear, "but
do you know the way to
Bluebell Meadow?"

"Just follow the
butterflies," Owl said.

Little Bear, Rabbit, and Mouse sat on
a rock and waited for butterflies.

And waited.

"I don't think we'll ever find Bluebell
Meadow," Little Bear said sadly.

Then something fluttered

past her nose.

"A butterfly!" squeaked Mouse.
"Quick!" cried Little Bear, jumping to her feet.

Little Bear, Rabbit, and Mouse
followed the butterfly through
the woods.

They followed it up the hill,
and down the other side.

And when they got to
the top of the next hill, they saw...

...a meadow of bluebells and

butterflies dancing in the sunlight.

"We found Bluebell Meadow!"
shouted Little Bear.

They played **hide-and-seek**
among the bluebells.

They played **peekaboo,**
and made daisy chains.

But mostly they chased the butterflies.

"This is the best day ever!" Rabbit said flopping on the grass.

"I could stay here forever," said Little Bear sleepily.

"Wake up! It's dinner time,"
said Mommy Bear.
Little Bear opened her eyes.

"But I've been to Bluebell Meadow
with Rabbit and Mouse," she said.

"It was just a dream," said Mommy Bear.
"It seemed so real!" said Little Bear.
"Good dreams are like that," Mommy Bear
said, giving her a great big bearhug.